BY ERIC A. KIMMEL

PICTURES BY PHIL HULING

Marshall Cavendish

New York London Singapore

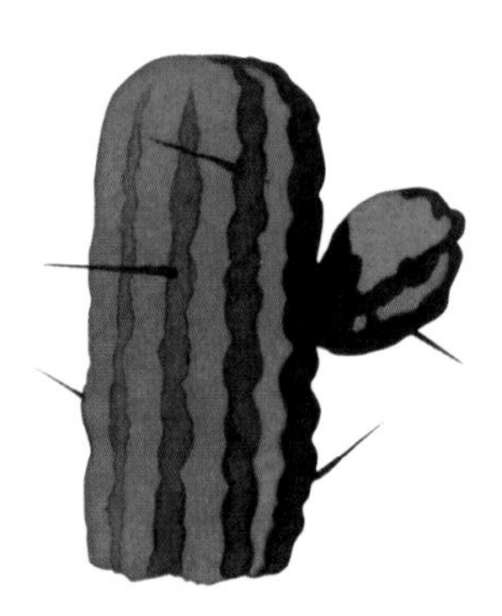

Marshall Cavendish, 99 White Plains Road, Tarrytown, NY 10591
www.marshallcavendish.com

Library of Congress Cataloging-in-Publication Data
Kimmel, Eric A.
Cactus soup / by Eric A. Kimmel ; illustrated by Phil Huling.— 1st ed.
p. cm.
Summary: During the Mexican Revolution, when a troop of hungry soldiers comes to a town where all the food has been hidden, they charm the townspeople into helping make a soup from water and a cactus thorn.

ISBN 0-7614-5155-2
[1. Folklore—France.] I. Huling, Phil, ill. II. Title.
PZ8.1.K567Cac 2004
398.2'0944'02—dc21
2003009110

The text of this book is set in Novarese Medium.

The illustrations are rendered in watercolor and inks on watercolor paper.

Printed in China

First edition

1 3 5 6 4 2

To Anna Cruz, Gloria Montalvo, and the

children of San Benito, Texas.

—E.A.K.

To Santiago, Ethel, Diego, Isabel,

and their soup angel, Juanita.

—P.H.

ONE DAY a troop of soldiers came riding toward the town of San Miguel.

Not everyone was happy to see them. "Soldiers are all alike, no matter whose side they fight on," the mayor grumbled. "They eat like wolves. There won't be a *tortilla* left when they get through!"

"What should we do?" the people asked.

"We'll do what we always do," said the mayor. "We'll hide our food and tell the soldiers we have nothing to give them. They'll leave when they see they aren't going to be fed."

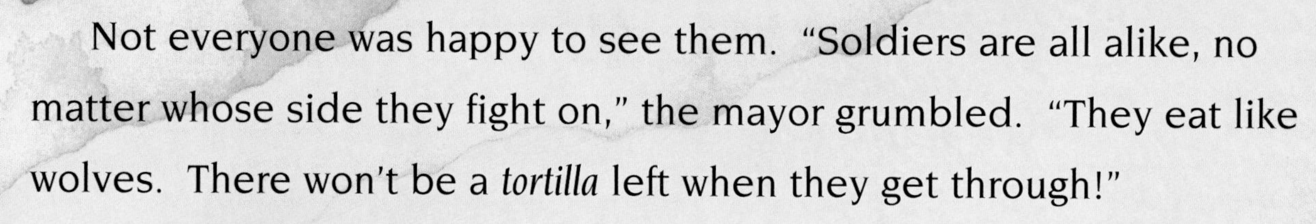

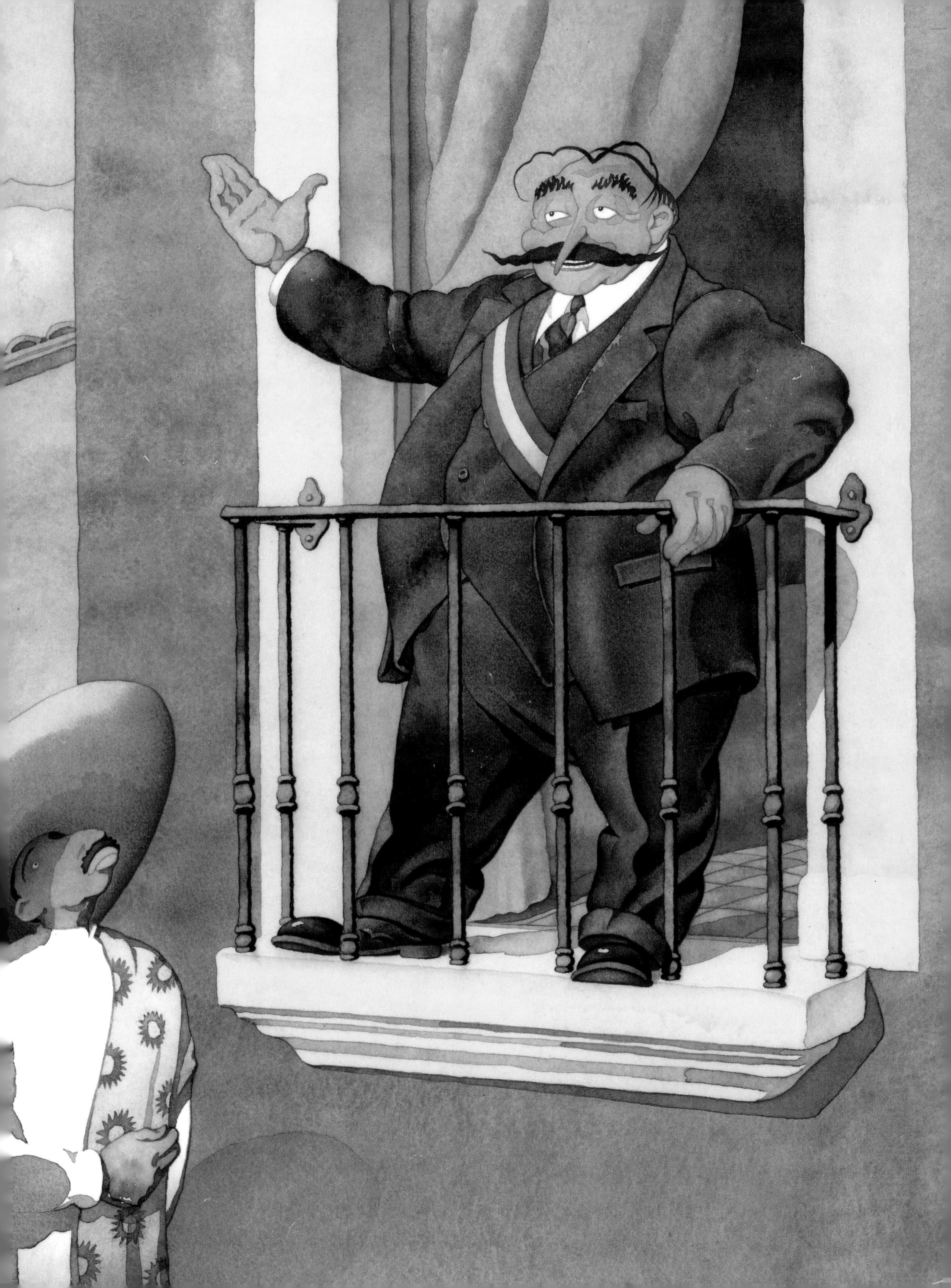

Everyone in San Miguel went to work. They buried sacks of beans and cornmeal in their gardens and lowered baskets of *tortillas* and *tamales* into the old stone well. Some hid chickens under their beds and ducks and geese in the bathtubs. Several carried pigs up to the rooftops while their neighbors herded cows and sheep into the cellars. The children hung strings of *chile* peppers high in the trees where no one would see them.

Once that was done, the townspeople put on torn, dirty clothes, smeared mud on their faces, and tried their best to look like poor, hungry people.

The soldiers came riding into town on prancing horses. They wore wide *sombreros*, with leather *bandoleras* slung across their chests. The captain saluted the mayor and townspeople.

"*Señor Alcalde*, my *compañeros* and I have been riding all day. We're tired and hungry. Can you spare some beans and *tortillas*? We would be so grateful."

The mayor frowned. "I am sorry, *Señor Capitán*. As you see, our town is very poor. Other soldiers came by the other day. They ate the few beans and *tortillas* we had. Now we have nothing. There isn't even enough for the little ones."

The parents nudged their children, who began crying bitterly, just as they had practiced.

"What a pity," the captain said. "Did you hear that, *amigos*? There's nothing to eat in this town. It looks like we're going to have to make cactus soup."

"Oh no!" the soldiers cried. "Not cactus soup *again*!"

"Stop complaining," the captain said. "Cactus soup is better than no soup at all."

The children stopped crying. Everyone in the plaza leaned forward to listen as the mayor asked, "What is cactus soup?"

"You'll see," said the captain. "I'll make enough for my soldiers and everyone in town. However, I'm going to need help. Can you bring me a kettle of water, a stirring spoon, plenty of firewood, and one cactus thorn? We have lots of people to feed, so bring the biggest thorn you can find."

The mayor ordered everyone to help. A kettle of water was soon boiling in the plaza. Cactus grew everywhere in town. The children had no trouble finding a huge thorn as long and as sharp as a needle.

"This thorn will make plenty of soup!" the captain exclaimed. He dropped it into the kettle and began stirring.

"How can anyone make soup from a cactus thorn?" asked the priest.

"Watch carefully. Perhaps we'll learn something," whispered the mayor.

The people of San Miguel looked on as the captain stirred. And stirred. And stirred. He lifted the spoon, blew on it, let it cool, had a taste. "Not bad," he declared, as he continued stirring. "I always find that a pinch or two of salt improves the flavor. But never mind. I know how poor you are. Why ask for what you don't have?"

"We have salt," said the mayor. "We're not as poor as that."

"And pepper, too," the town clerk added. "Does cactus soup taste good with *chiles*?"

"Cactus soup is outstanding with *chiles*!" the soldiers exclaimed.

People tripped over themselves running home to fetch salt. The children climbed trees to bring down strings of *chile* peppers. The captain stirred the salt and *chiles* into the soup. He took another taste.

"It's getting better," he declared. "Too bad you don't have onions. Cactus soup always tastes better with onions. But why ask for what you don't have?"

"I know where I can find some onions," said the priest.

"What about garlic?" asked the sacristan.

"Garlic makes excellent soup," the captain answered. The priest and the sacristan ran to the church. They came back a few minutes later with a sack of onions and several heads of garlic. The captain chopped up the vegetables and dropped them into the kettle.

"Smell that soup!" he exclaimed, as he continued stirring.

The people of San Miguel sniffed the air. "Soup that smells this good must taste wonderful!" cried the members of the town council.

"If only we had some beans. And carrots. And tomatoes. And perhaps even a fat stewing hen. Then our soup would really have flavor," said the captain. "But it's fine the way it is. Why ask for what you don't have?"

The townspeople winked at each other. "Come with us," they told the soldiers. They returned in a few minutes, carrying sacks of beans, bunches of carrots, baskets of tomatoes, and several fat stewing hens.

"The hens were old," said the mayor. "They wouldn't have lived much longer."

"The tomatoes were spoiled," said the barber.

"The beans were rotten," said the school teacher.

"The carrots were moldy," said the shoemaker.

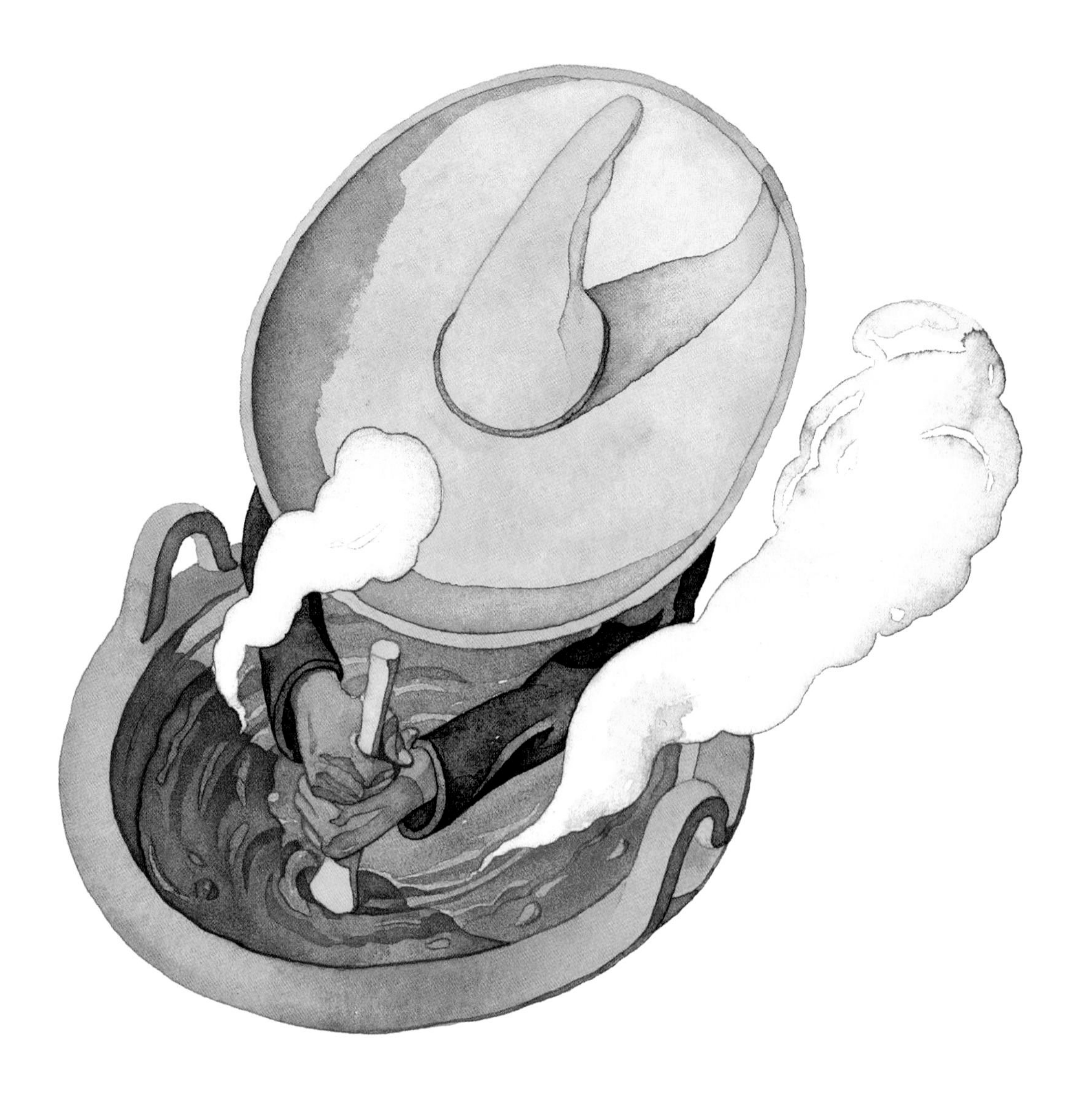

"Never mind," said the captain, as he stirred and stirred the ingredients into the thick, rich soup. "That's the best part of cactus soup. Whatever you add makes it taste good. Mmm! I think it's ready now. Who wants to try some?"

"Me!" Everyone lined up in the plaza, bowls in hand. The captain ladled out the soup.

"This is the best soup I ever ate!" said the mayor.

"I never tasted anything like it!" said his wife.

"And to think it was made from a cactus thorn!" exclaimed the priest.

"Not bad!" said the captain. "However, I think cactus soup always tastes better when you have something to go with it."

"Such as?" all the people asked.

"*Tortillas*! *Tamales*! Sweet potatoes! A roasting pig!" cried the soldiers.

"That would make for a real *fiesta*," the captain said. "And some music, too, for dancing later on. However, I know how poor you are. Why ask for what you don't have?"

"Wait here," the mayor told the soldiers. He whispered orders to everyone in town. They all ran home—and came back carrying *tortillas*, *tamales*, *chorizo*, *camotes*, and several fat roasting pigs.

What a feast they had! As the night wore on, soldiers and towns-people ate until they couldn't hold another bite. Then they brought out accordions and guitars for singing and dancing.

The *fiesta* lasted until dawn. Nobody in town could remember anything like it.

The soldiers rode away in the morning. The people of San Miguel gathered in the plaza to wave good-bye.

"What will we do if more soldiers come?" they asked the mayor, when the last soldier disappeared from sight.

"Let them come, the more the better," the mayor replied. "Feeding soldiers is no trouble. We can feed a whole army and have a *fiesta* every night, as long as we remember how to make . . .

Cactus Soup!

Pancho Villa

Emiliano Zapata

Author's Note

The story of "Stone Soup" or "Nail Soup" appears in cultures around the world. I chose to set this version in the time of the Mexican Revolution, which lasted from 1910 to 1922. Under leaders such as Pancho Villa and Emiliano Zapata, the common people of Mexico struggled to take back political and economic power from the wealthy classes and foreign business interests that controlled most of the country.

  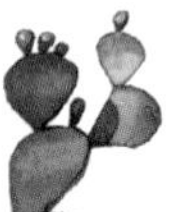 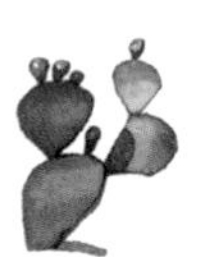 

Glossary

Alcalde – mayor.

Amigos – friends.

Bandoleras – belts, usually worn across the chest, with small loops for holding bullets.

Camote – sweet potato.

Capitán – captain.

Chile – one of several kinds of hot peppers.

Chorizo – sausage.

Compañeros – companions.

Fiesta – festival.

Señor – "Sir" or "Master."

Sombrero – Straw or felt hat with a wide, circular brim.

Tamale – spicy Mexican dish made of chopped meat and fried, crushed peppers. This mixture is rolled in cornmeal, wrapped in cornhusks, and steamed.

Tortilla – round, flat bread made from cornmeal or flour and baked on a hot stone or griddle.

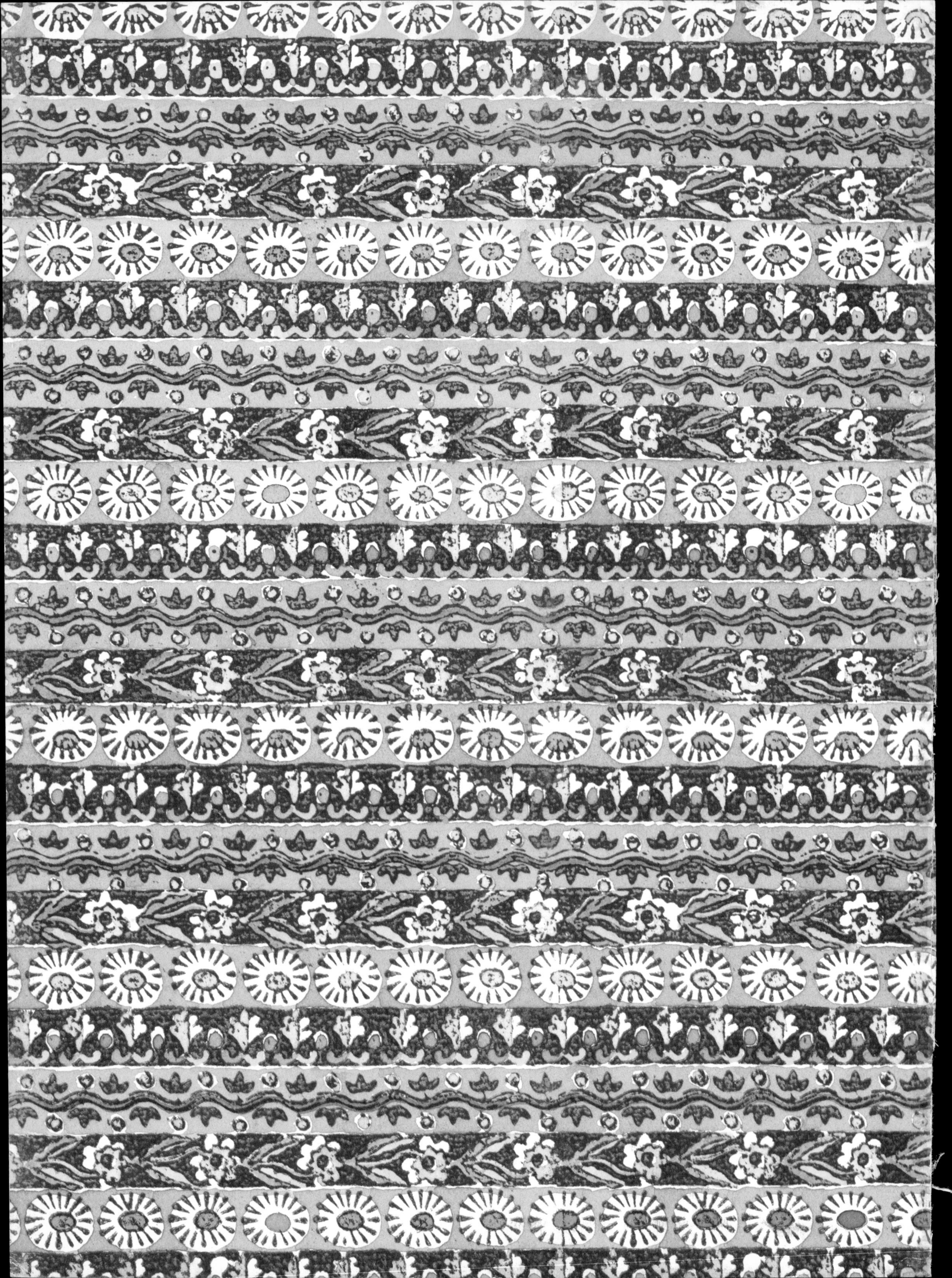

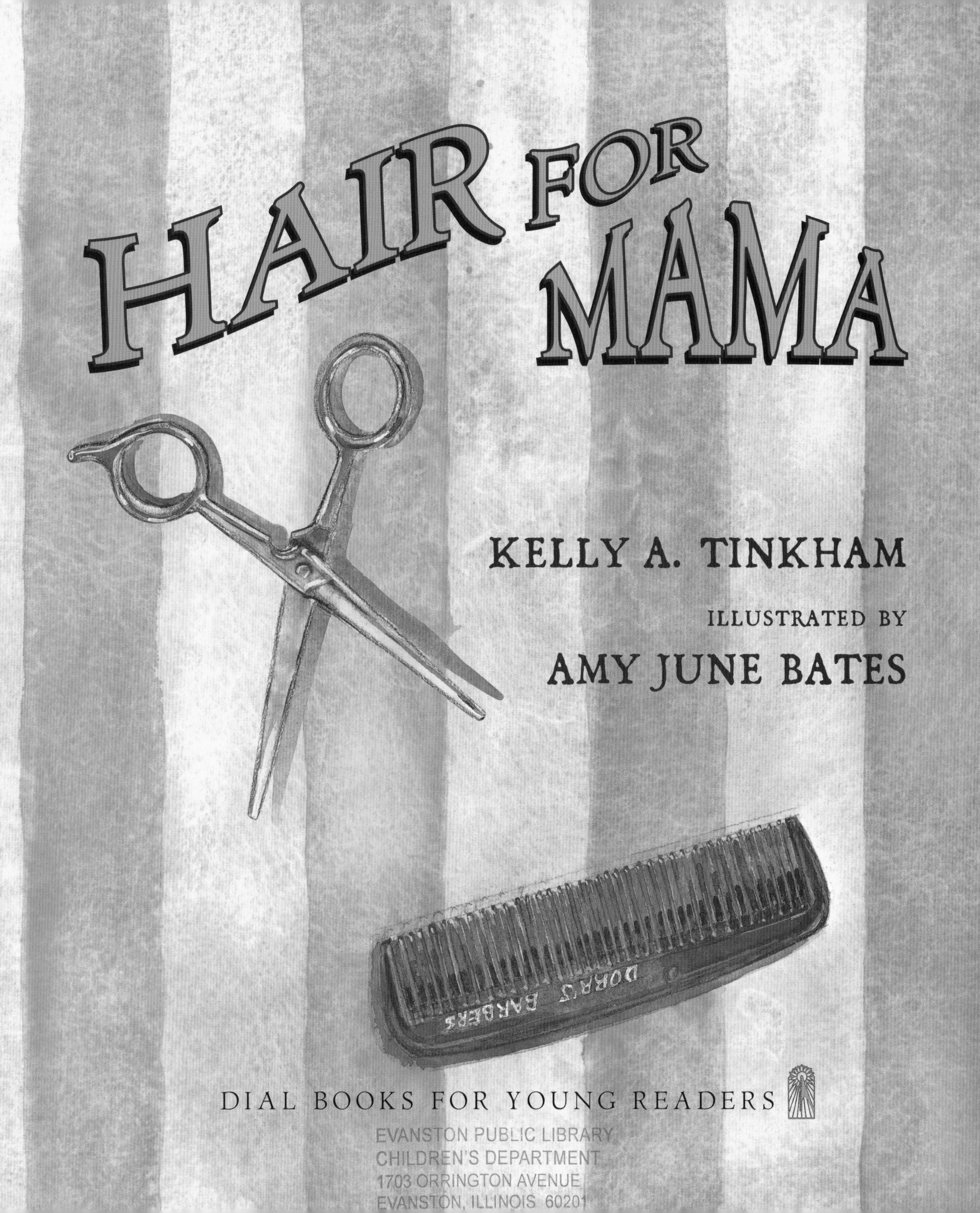

HAIR FOR MAMA

KELLY A. TINKHAM

ILLUSTRATED BY

AMY JUNE BATES

DIAL BOOKS FOR YOUNG READERS

Most folks don't know how important hair is. But I do. Hair has always been important to us Carters, especially in October on picture day. I look best in a fade. My sister, Yolanda, likes braids and beads. Little Stevie and Papa have short, natural hairdos. And Mama keeps her hair long and braided. Except on picture day, when she loops and gathers her braids together like a beautiful black crown.

But that changed back in August. Mama got cancer.

Mama said cancer was a disease. Some small part inside her was growing too quickly and too big and was crowding out other parts she needed. Sounded to me like the weeds growing in Mama's flower garden—crowding out the marigolds, petunias, and snapdragons.

Mama said she would take a medicine called chemotherapy. The medicine worked to stop the cancer from growing, but she might feel sick and tired . . . and lose her crown of hair.

All September I watched Mama brush her hair thinner every day. "Mm-mm-mm," she said one morning. "Seems I'm shedding even more than Sophie."

Sophie was our cat. "Oh Mama," I told her, knowing she missed her braids, "even if you lose all your hair, I'll find you more."

Mama pointed her brush at me. "How you going to do that, Marcus?"

"I don't know," I admitted, "but I will."

By October that promise had slipped my mind. Picture day was coming! Papa had hired Midge Larsen to photograph us under the trees at Crawford Park. Mama loved those fire-red maples, blaze-orange sassafras, and golden-yellow beech. "Best trees in Moline County," she always said.

But this year Mama hardly noticed the trees. When I showed her a sugar maple red as a cardinal, she was so tired all she managed to say was, "Mm-hmm." By now her head was bare and when she smiled, her eyes still looked sad. Like mine did last year when my favorite cousin, Richy, moved to Virginia.

I worried even more when picture day was five days away and Mama hadn't taken us shopping for clothes. I decided to talk to Yolanda. She was ten, two years older than me.

"Mama's sick," she said. "Real sick."

My promise sneaked into my mind. I couldn't help saying, "Nothing a little hair won't solve."

Yolanda rolled her eyes. "It's not that simple, Marcus. Some people don't get better."

"Mama will," I said. "She's taking medicine. She'll get better."

That Monday night I asked Mama about picture day. She felt queasy and was resting in the chair while Papa cooked supper. Her face was puffy and pale.

"We'll have pictures," she said, squinting at me, "but I don't think I want to be in them. Me with no hair . . . I don't have the heart to see a picture of myself with no hair."

Yolanda dropped her book and leaned on Mama's chair. "It won't be the same without you," she pleaded. "You can wear a gele. No one will know you're bare underneath."

"I'll know. I'll know I have no hair." Mama got a faraway look in her eyes, and she said, "I don't want to be remembered that way."

It didn't seem right Mama not being in the pictures. "I'll find you hair," I told her.

Yolanda rolled her eyes again. Mama didn't say anything. She only smiled and went back to dozing.

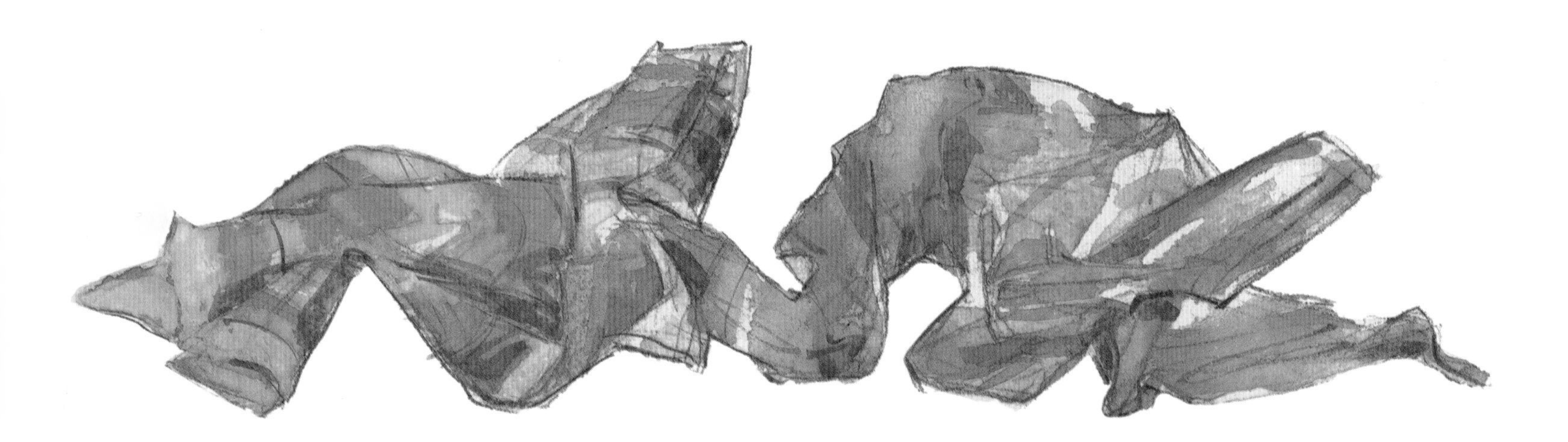

All the next day I kept my thinking cap buckled, working on finding hair. After school Mama took us shopping at DeWitt's department store. "You go on ahead," she said. "I'll be along shortly." We headed straight for the toys, though we didn't make it that far.

I stopped at the Halloween aisle. It was full of costumes, masks, and something else.

"Look!" I said. "Hair. Wigs of hair."

Yolanda and I snatched several. "Try these on," I told Mama.

"I don't know." She hesitated until even Yolanda begged. After looking around, Mama knelt and took off her hat. I helped pull a wig on her head.

"Well?" she said. "Am I beautiful?"

"Too red." I laid the doll hair down.

Yolanda tried witch hair. "Too gray." The scarecrow hair was too poky, and the clown wig too colorful. Seemed the afro was closest to Mama's real hair, but not quite right either.

I was about to try another when Mama took my hands in hers. "Marcus, Mama can't wear these costume wigs. I don't feel like myself in them. I feel like a striped tiger dressing up in spots. Do you understand what I'm saying?"

I nodded. Inside my heart felt tighter than the knots Papa made when he tied my shoes. I knew if I was to find hair Mama would wear, it would have to be something special.

The week slipped by. Soon it was Friday evening before picture day and the knots in my heart were harder than ever. Mama was worn out all the time, but I couldn't sleep. Finally I drifted off that night praying for a double miracle—that Mama would be in the family pictures and get better.

OPEN

Next morning the sunrise set the trees on fire with color. Mama fixed Yolanda's braids. Papa used a pick on his and Stevie's dos. But I wasn't a bit closer to finding hair for Mama.

After breakfast, Papa dropped me at the barber shop while he ran Saturday errands. "Tell Mr. Dorr to freshen your fade," he told me. "Not too short."

Mr. Dorr was cutting a man's hair. Clip, clip, clip. Hair tumbled to the floor. I glanced once—then twice—at the pile around Mr. Dorr's shoes. That's when I knew exactly what I needed to do.

Mr. Dorr called me to the chair. "How's your mama been?"

I didn't know what to say, so I answered, "She's coming along fine." I wanted him to hurry and cut before Papa came back.

"Good," said Mr. Dorr. "Need your usual today?"

"Nope." I hoped Mr. Dorr wouldn't question me too much. "Trim it all off, please."

"Now Marcus, you always get a fade." He reached for the telephone. "I better call your mama."

"No!" I said. "Mama's resting. Papa dropped me off. Told me to tell you what I needed."

Mr. Dorr let the phone rest. "All right, Marcus. Hope I don't get into hot water for this."

I sat stock-still while the trimmer hummed. Mama would have hair! She would be in the pictures and get better.

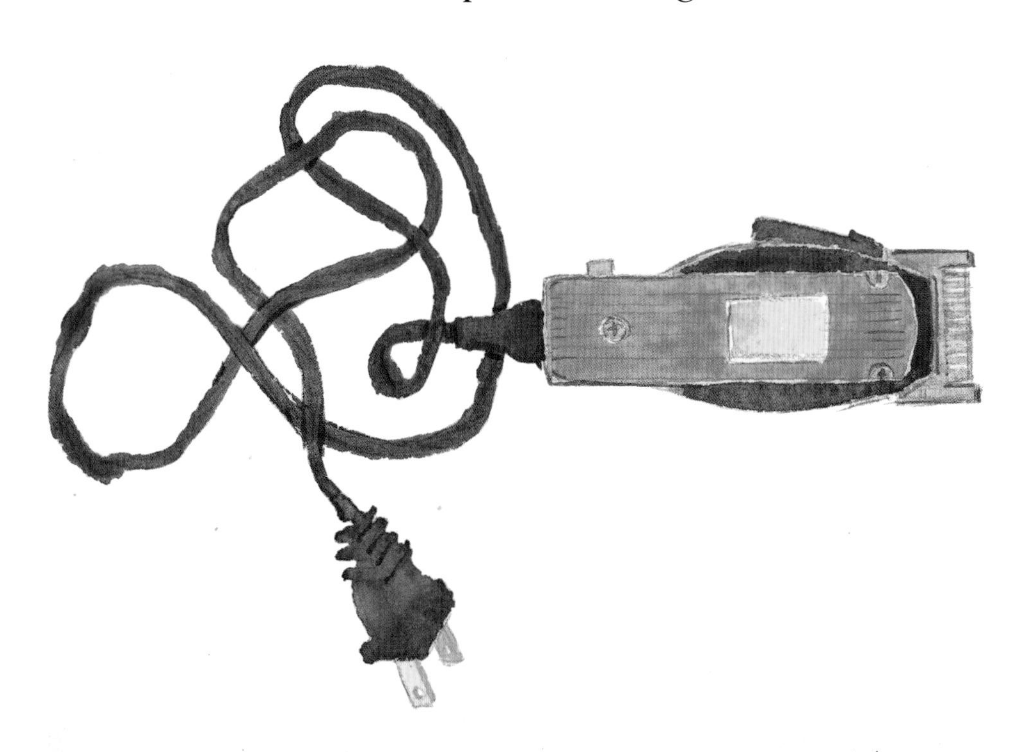

Dorr's

Soon Mr. Dorr whirled me toward the mirror. "All done, boy." I couldn't believe my eyes. I looked different—like Mama. I must have sat staring longer than I realized, because when I finally looked, the floor was clean!

"Where's my hair?" I was frantic. "I need it!"

Mr. Dorr laughed. "You don't want your hair, Marcus. Been on the floor. I swept it into the trash with everyone else's."

I burst into tears. My plan hadn't given me a single hair. I cried until Papa came.

"Marcus?" said Papa. "What happened?"

I couldn't stop crying to answer. Mr. Dorr tried to explain. Papa pulled me close. "What's going on, son?"

"Hair." I gulped. "Mama needed hair. I cut mine to give to her." I sucked in another breath. "But Mr. Dorr threw it away." Now I was sobbing. Papa said good-bye to Mr. Dorr and took me home.

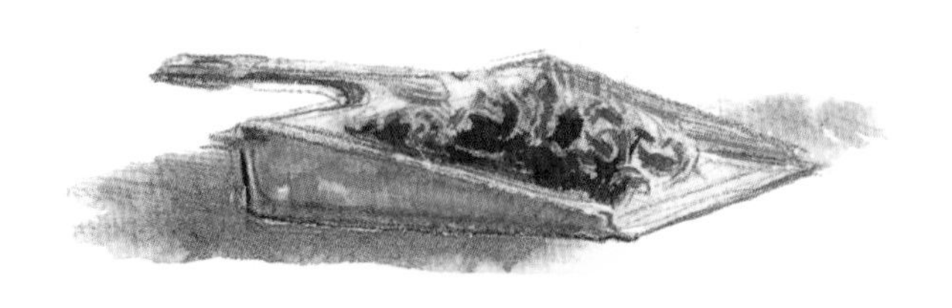

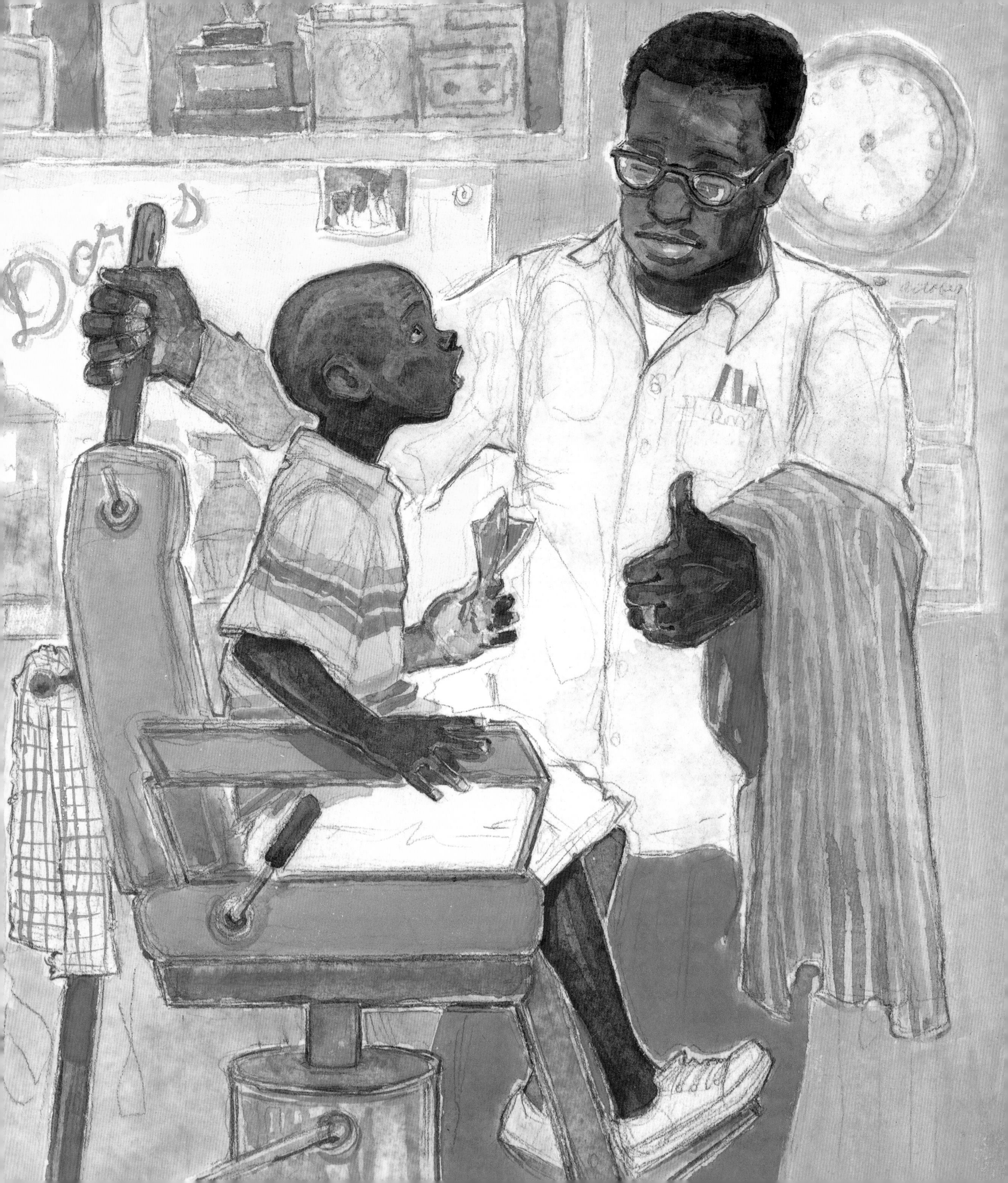

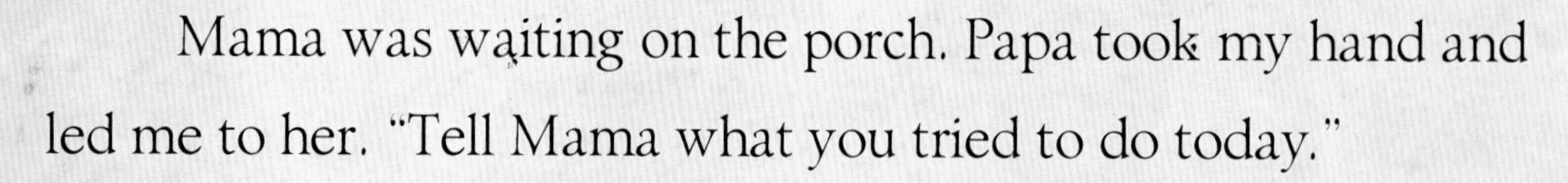

Mama was waiting on the porch. Papa took my hand and led me to her. "Tell Mama what you tried to do today."

Nervously I told her the story. She didn't say a word. Her lips were squeezed tight, and her eyes glistened like cups of water ready to spill.

"I'm sorry, Mama. Sorry I lost your hair."

"Baby, you didn't lose anything." Mama held my face between her hands. "I don't need hair when I have you!"

"But without hair, you won't get better!" I said. "Who will be my mama if you go away?"

"Oh, Marcus," she said. "Finding me hair wouldn't make me better or worse. Though I don't like being this way, it does mean the medicine is working hard inside me to stop the cancer. And the doctor says I'm making progress." Mama slipped her arm around me. "But I promise I will never stop being your mama because I'll always be with you in your heart. My love wraps itself around you and won't ever let go."

"No matter what?" I asked.

"No matter what," she said.

I hugged Mama so tight that those knots in my heart loosened and fell away. Soon we had a family bear hug. And I knew we would meet whatever happened down the road together.

Before leaving for the park, Mama said, "Wait a minute," and ran inside the house. When she came back she had a gele wrapped around her head—just like Yolanda had suggested. "Now let's get some family pictures taken," she said. She was smiling.

That afternoon Midge photographed us by the Crawford River. Mama said the trees were wearing their best colors like us. And a month later my hair was growing back fine.

Three months later Mama came home from the doctor with good news.

"The chemotherapy is working. In six weeks the treatments will be done. At least for now, no more cancer."

"Yippee!" We whooped and hollered around the house.

Mama took me in her arms and rubbed the fuzz growing on my head. "What do you say Mama try a little hair again too?"

"I say YES." Hair was nice to have. But not as nice as me having Mama and Mama having me.

Papa said soon as the dogwood trees bloomed, we were starting a new Carter tradition—family pictures in May! Think I'll try a new hairstyle. Wonder what Mama will think of me with braids . . .